This book belongs to

....

www.makebelieveideas.com

Written by Alexandra Robinson.
Illustrated by Clare Fennell.

SANTA'S 12 DAYS OF CHRISTMAS

Clare Fennell • Alexandra Robinson

make
believe
ideas

Have **you** ever **wondered**
what **Santa** likes to do
when his **deliveries** are done,
and **Christmas Eve** is through?

Welcome Back!

He lands his sleigh on Christmas day, greeted by a cheer.
He's ready for a twelve-day break – it's been a busy year!

On **DAY 1** of his holidays
he throws a **yuletide ball**,
with **disco lights**, **red party hats**
and **candy canes** for all!

On **DAY 2**, Santa takes the **train** through the **sparkling snow**.

He's off to see The Nutcracker –
his favourite Christmas show!

On DAY 3, jolly Mr C

holds a reindeer race.

The elves stand by and watch with glee

to see who wins first place!

Finish

On DAY 4, Santa Claus decides to skate with polar bears.

They Swirl and Swish around the ice . . . and leap into the air!

On DAY 5, Santa takes his wife
to watch the town parade.
They cheer The Mince Pie Marching Band
and praise The Dance Brigade!

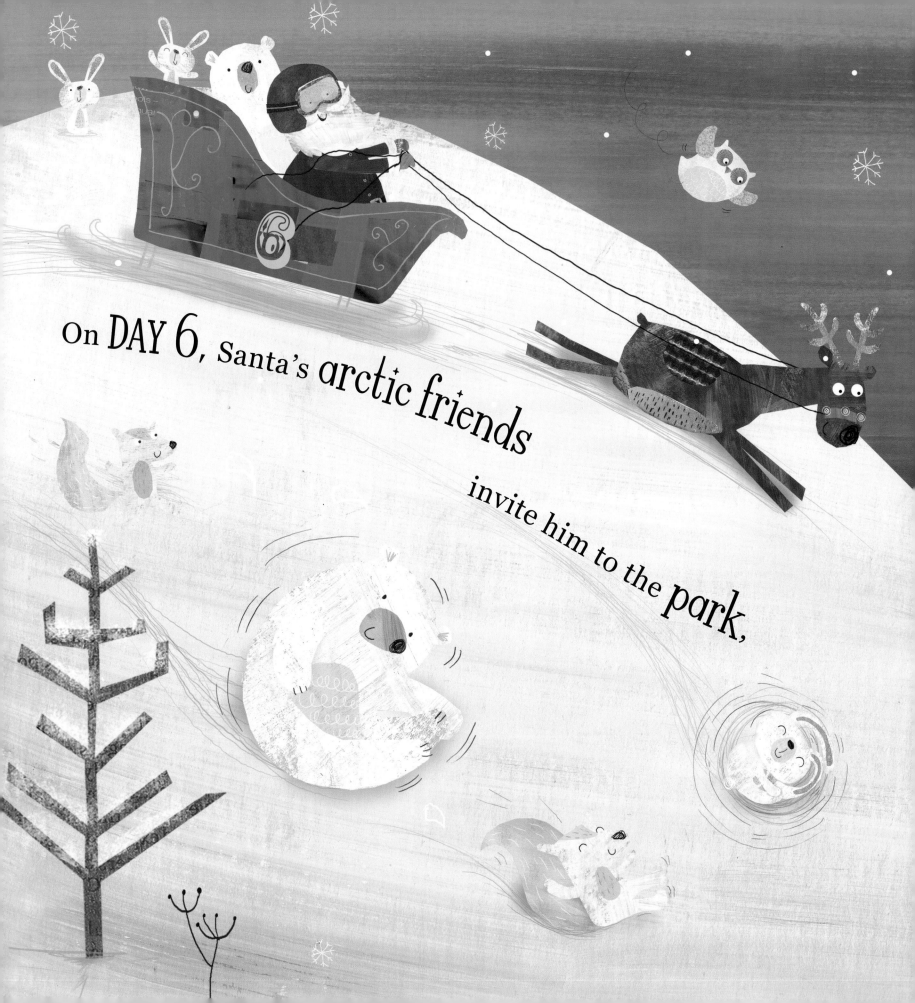

On **DAY 6**, Santa's arctic friends invite him to the **park**,

where, down the hill, they sledge and slide
until the sky turns dark!

On New Year's Eve, the 7th DAY,

they all watch with delight

as fireworks WHIZZ, POP

and BANG,

filling the sky with light!

On DAY 8, Santa takes some wool
and dazzling glitter gems,
then settles in his chair to knit
warm jumpers for his friends!

On DAY 9, Santa and the elves enjoy the frosty weather.

They play **snow games**,

build tall **snowmen**

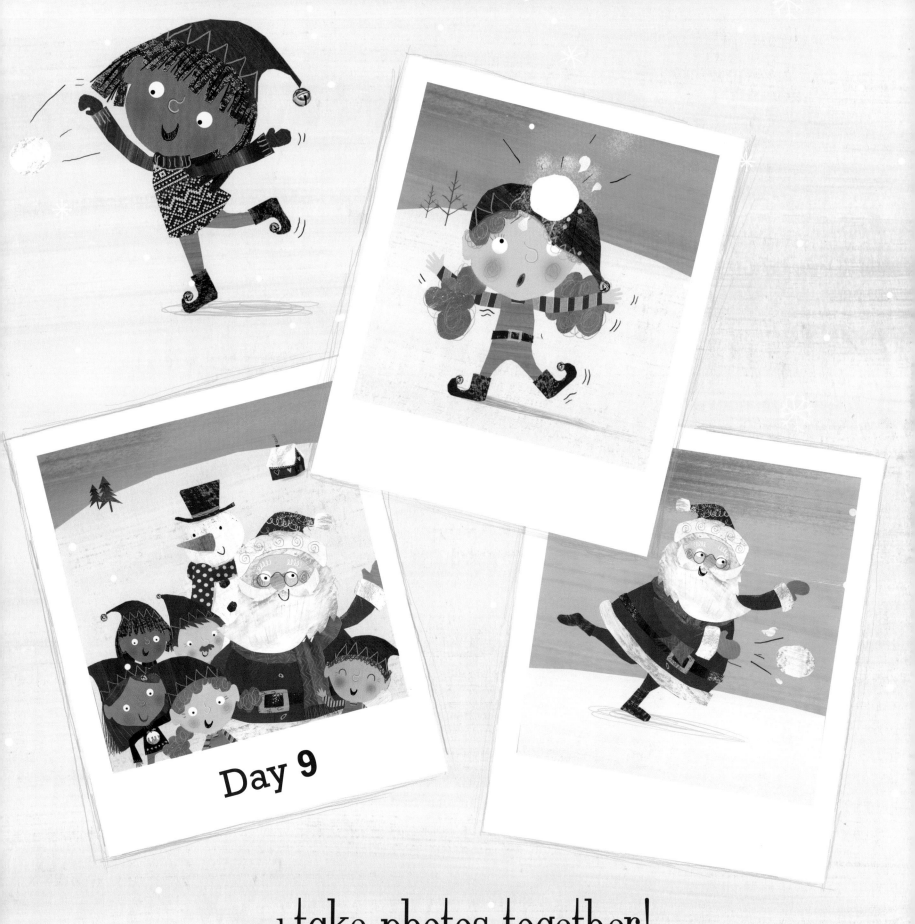

Day 9

and take photos together!

On DAY 10, Santa plans to try
some recipes he's read:
three cream tarts, two fruit soufflés
and a house of gingerbread!

On **DAY 11**, Santa Claus
prepares a **roaring fire**,
then **sings** some **merry carols** with
The Rockin' Robin Choir!

On **DAY 12** of his festive break,
he **polishes** his sleigh.

He's **ready to start** making plans
for **next year's Christmas Day!**

DAY 1

DAY 2

DAY 3

DAY 4

DAY 5

DAY 6

DAY 7

DAY 8

DAY 9

DAY 10

DAY 11

DAY 12